ANGEL

The Hollower

ANGEL
The Hollower

based on the television series
Buffy the Vampire Slayer™
created by
JOSS WHEDON

writer
CHRISTOPHER GOLDEN

penciller
HECTOR GOMEZ

inker
SANDU FLOREA

colorist
GUY MAJOR

letterer
KEN BRUZENAK

DARK HORSE COMICS

publisher
MIKE RICHARDSON

editor
SCOTT ALLIE
with ADAM GALLARDO *and* BEN ABERNATHY

collection designer
KEITH WOOD

art director
MARK COX

Special thanks to
DEBBIE OLSHAN *at Fox Licensing,*
CAROLINE KALLAS *and* GEORGE SNYDER *at*
Buffy the Vampire Slayer, and
DAVID CAMPITI *at Glass House Graphics.*

Published by
Dark Horse Comics, Inc.
10956 SE Main Street
Milwaukie, OR 97222

First edition: May 2000
ISBN: 1-56971-450-9

1 3 5 7 9 10 8 6 4 2

Printed in Canada.

Introduction

To put *The Hollower* in perspective, we've got to move back on the chronoscale to a time when *Angel*, as a television series and spinoff of *Buffy the Vampire Slayer*, didn't exist. Though we became aware of it during the process of developing *The Hollower*, editor Scott Allie and I had talked about doing a miniseries focusing on the brooding, soulful vampire who had become the most popular supporting character on *Buffy*.

I admit, I had my reservations.

Chief among those was that Angel shares certain character similarities with Peter Octavian, the main character of my own *Shadow Saga* series of novels. Lord, I wish people would stop pointing this out as though I were unaware of it. For the record, Octavian was created in 1988, and first saw print in 1994.

Thus, I hesitated to write about Angel by virtue of the logic that I might be tempted to create stories I might better use to my advantage later in writing about Octavian.

After ruminating on that for a while, however, I realized I was being a bit silly and simple-minded about it all. After all, Angel exists in the universe of Joss Whedon's singularly brilliant creation, *Buffy the Vampire Slayer*. As long as I worked within the structure of that universe, I reasoned, no way would I end up with anything remotely resembling my previous original work.

The book you hold in your hand is testament to that.

Before I continue, I must note that comics is a collaborative medium. A great many fine people at Dark Horse, Fox, and Mutant Enemy — as well as a very talented art team — contributed to the creation *Angel: The Hollower*. The final product reflects their hard work, particularly that of editor Scott Allie.

So, back to Angel.

When I sat down to come up with a story for the very first *Angel* miniseries, there were three agendas at work: mine, editor Scott Allie's, and that of the people at the *Buffy* office, including Joss Whedon himself, and the licensing team at Fox and Mutant Enemy, Debbie Olshan and Caroline Kallas.

Their agenda indicated that the story needed to not only include *Buffy*, but have an impact on her. Of course, I had no problem with that.

Previously, I had only been able to write *Buffy* (in comics — I had already co-authored a number of the *Buffy* novels) in small doses in *The Origin*, a five page *TV Guide* story, and the *Buffy* #1/2 limited edition. The impact would be played out with a question: how far will Angel go if offered a chance, no matter how slim, at a normal life with Buffy? And how far will Buffy allow him to go?

Scott's agenda was to highlight evil Angel as well as good Angel since fans love both faces of the character. Again, not a problem. Angelus is gloriously evil; which is always fun. Scott and I agreed not only to highlight evil Angel, but to create an entire second story, told in flashbacks, that would introduce the threat and would also include two of my favorite characters, Spike and Drusilla.

Finally, my agenda. First, I wanted to explore the dichotomy between what Angel was, and what he has become, both in the sense of his relationship to other vampires, and his relationship to Buffy. The presence of a former vampire lover, and of the Hollower, drew those questions sharply into focus, creating a pair of philosophical challenges for Angel (which I won't go into here — don't want to ruin the story).

Second, as long as I could fulfill everyone else's expectations at the same time, my most profound desire was to create an enemy, a monster, who would frighten vampires. A bogeyman for vampires, if you will. It was the perfect way to marry the evil Angel story line with the present day "good" Angel story . . . bring in a creature which was the only natural predator of vampires other than the Slayer.

The Hollower was born.

I hope you find him as creepy as I did. While you're reading, though, ask yourself this: in Angel's position, what would *you* do?

CHRISTOPHER GOLDEN
Bradford, Massachusetts

Sunnydale, California. Number one tourist destination for wayward vampires and other assorted monsters.
It falls to Buffy Summers, the Slayer, to try and deter this kind of tourism. Sometimes she has help. More often than not, that help includes Angel, the vampire with whom she has fallen in love.
He has his own history.
CURSED!
I'M SORRY, ANGELUS. I DON'T KNOW WHAT'S HAPPENED TO YOU, BUT IF YOU'RE WILLING TO KILL YOUR OWN KIND...YOU'RE DUST.
YOU NEED ANY HELP, ANGEL?
THANKS, BUT I'VE GOT IT.
YOU DON'T KNOW ME, DORIAN, YOU ONLY KNOW THE MONSTER I USED TO BE.

A vampire is, in essence, a human corpse with a demon inside.

In Angel's case, however, the demon within shares residence with his own soul.
YOU KNEW THAT ONE, DIDN'T YOU? FROM... BEFORE. ARE YOU ALL RIGHT?
As punishment for the abominations he had committed as a vampire, a gypsy clan gave him back his soul, so that he would live with the horror and guilt of what he'd done.

A demon with all the memories and much of the personality of the corpse.

NEVER.
SHE REMINDED YOU OF THE PAST, BUT THAT WASN'T YOU, ANGEL. YOU DIDN'T REALLY DO ALL OF THOSE THINGS, IT WAS THE DEMON. YOU KNOW THAT.
BUT IT WAS ME. THESE HANDS, THIS FLESH, THIS MIND, REALLY, IF YOU WANT TO THINK OF IT LIKE THAT.

It takes up residence where the soul used to be.

"I COULD LIVE UNTIL THE END OF THE WORLD, AND I'LL NEVER FORGET THE THINGS I DID."
Galway, Ireland. 1753.
"I HAD BEEN OUT CAROUSING WITH LIAM McHUGH, MY CLOSEST FRIEND, WHEN DARLA FOUND ME AND TOOK MY BLOOD."
WAKE NOW, ANGELUS, MY ANGEL. THE FIRST NIGHT OF FOREVER.
"SHE PROMISED ME ETERNITY, AND I WAS FOOLISH ENOUGH NOT TO ASK WHAT IT WOULD COST."
I... I CAN'T BREATHE!
FOOLISH BOY, YOU DON'T NEED TO BREATHE. NOT ANYMORE.
NOW COME, YOU MUST SAY GOODBYE TO YOUR OLD LIFE AND EMBRACE THE NEW. WE'LL BEGIN WITH A FEAST.
YOU MUST BE STARVED.

"I'D BEEN MISSING TWO NIGHTS BY THEN. LIAM WAS GREATLY CONCERNED. HE FELT RESPONSIBLE IN SOME WAY, I THINK, POOR BASTARD."
LOOK, IT WERE ONLY TWO NIGHTS AGO, HE WAS HERE WITH ME. I JUST WANT TO KNOW IF YE'VE SEEN HIM SINCE.
ARE YE DAFT, YE WEE LAD? AH'VE NOT SEEN HIM. DON'T KNOW I'D RECOGNIZE HIM IF I DID. NOW OFF WITH YE, IF YE'RE NOT PLANNING TO DRINK THIS EVENIN'.
AH, ANGELUS. WHAT HAVE YOU GOTTEN YERSELF INTO NOW?
LIAM, YE CAME LOOKING FOR ME.
NOW YE'VE FOUND ME.
SWEET, ISN'T IT? A HAPPY LITTLE REUNION.

"HE MEANT NOTHING TO ME, BUFFY. I LOOKED IN HIS FACE, AND ALL I SAW WAS THE BLOOD. MY HUNGER."
YE'VE GOT A LOT OF EXPLAINING TO DO, ME FRIEND. THOUGH I'D SAY THIS FINE LASS GOES A LONG WAY TOWARD THAT EXPLANATION.
YE HAVE NO IDEA HOW RIGHT YE ARE.
SAY, ARE YE ALL RIGHT, ANGELUS? YE DON'T LOOK QUITE RIGHT.
I FEEL WONDERFUL, LIAM. AND, AS FOR THAT WEE LASS YE EYED SO THOROUGHLY, HER NAME IS DARLA. SHE'S INTRODUCED ME TO A WHOLE NEW WORLD.
LET ME SHOW YOU.
AAAH!

"IT WAS... I ENJOYED IT THOROUGHLY, HIS FEAR, THE SCENT OF BLOOD. I TOYED WITH HIM, BUFFY, AND IT WAS FUN."
LORD HELP ME, ANGELUS. I DON'T KNOW WHAT YE'RE ABOUT...
...OR WHAT THAT SLATTERN HAS DONE TO YOUR MIND...
...BUT I'LL NOT WASTE ANOTHER MOMENT WITH YOU.
OH, DON'T RUN OFF YET, LIAM. THE NIGHT IS YOUNG, AND WE HAVEN'T EVEN EATEN YET.
OUT OF MY WAY, TROLLOP!
THAT ISN'T VERY NICE, LIAM.
DAMN YE TO HELL, ANGELUS. I'LL KILL YE FOR THAT.
I'VE NO DOUBT THAT YE WOULD...

...IF YE COULD.

GOD HELP ME, WHAT ARE YE?

GOD'S NOT LISTENING, LIAM.
AND, "WHAT AM I?," AMONG OTHER THINGS,...I'M HUNGRY.

THAT'S IT, MY BEAUTY. MY WEE LAD. YOU KNOW JUST WHAT TO DO.

"DARLA AND BLOOD, THOSE WERE MY ONLY PASSIONS. TOGETHER, WE SWEPT ACROSS EUROPE, BRINGING DEATH AND TERROR WHEREVER WE WENT."

I HAD THE TIME OF MY LIFE.

I KNOW IT HURTS, ANGEL, BUT THAT WAS BEFORE YOU HAD YOUR SOUL RESTORED. THAT WASN'T YOU.
I KNOW THE GUILT TEARS YOU APART, AND I KNOW THE MEMORIES MUST BE HORRIFYING FOR YOU...

BUFFY, YOU STILL DON'T GET IT, DO YOU? THERE'S MORE TO THE CURSE THAN GUILT.

ALL THOSE THINGS I DID... WHILE IT WAS HAPPENING, IT WAS SHEER PLEASURE, EVERY MINUTE OF IT.

MUCH AS IT SICKENS ME...

...THEY'RE GOOD MEMORIES.

ANDREW WONG

THE END

San Francisco, California.
Perhaps more than any other city in America, it's a place where everyone is welcome, and anything can happen.
A city of freedom, and new beginnings.
Under its lights, we are all free to pursue our dreams...
...or nightmares.
WELL, AIN'T THEY ADORABLE?
I WOULD HAVE SAID "DELECTABLE," BUT HAVE IT YOUR WAY.
AHHH! NO, WHAT DO YOU THINK YOU'RE--
I LOVE THIS CITY, JOHNNY LEE, SO MANY FLAVORS.
NO! OH, GOD, LET ME GOOOOO!
DAMN! COME BACK HERE, YA LITTLE--

NOOO! GET AWAY!
I DON'T LIKE TO WORK FOR MY FOOD, GIRL. I'M GONNA HAVE TO DO YOU MESSY, NOW.
Mmmmmm. ROMANCE, THE SPICE OF LIFE.
NOW, WHERE DID THAT BOY RUN OFF TO...?
THAT'S FAR ENOUGH!
NO! GET YOUR HANDS OFF ME, YOU--OH, NO, PLEASE--
AH, THERE YOU ARE! WHAT A GLORIOUS NIGHT, LOVER. WE'RE LIKE WOLVES IN THE PRIMEVAL FOREST, RUNNING THE PREY TO GROUND.
I LOVE THIS TOWN!
SHAKK!

YES, BABY! GIVE ME THAT REBEL YELL AGAIN! I GET CHILLS EVERY TIME. THAT YELL'S WHAT MADE ME FALL FOR YOU BACK WHEN YOU WERE HUMAN.

YEEEE-HAAAA!

HAA-!

JOHNNY LEE! NO! NOT YOU, BABY! NOOOO!

IT CAN'T BE! NOT HERE! NOT NOW! I DON'T THINK I HAVE THE STRENGTH TO FIGHT IT AGAIN.

Sunnydale, California.
NELSON KENT
1935-1998
ACCEPTED THIS FATE
Two months later.
NO, REALLY, I MEAN IT, I'M THE CHOSEN ONE, PAL. THE SLAYER. ONE GIRL IN ALL THE WORLD CHOSEN TO FIGHT THE HORDES OF DARKNESS. BLAH BLAH BLAH. YOU KNOW THE DRILL.
SO, YOU'VE GOTTA TRUST ME ON THIS...
UHNFF!
CRACK
...EVEN FOR A CHAOS DEMON, YOU ARE ONE OF THE UGLIEST SONS OF--
YOUR PRATTLING BETRAYS YOUR FEAR, CHILD.
THAT'S NOT FEAR, YOU IDIOT...
UNGGHH!
WHUMP!
...IT'S CONFIDENCE.
YOU'RE BOTH WRONG. IT'S NOT FEAR AND IT'S NOT CONFIDENCE

IT'S "I-HAVE-A-TEST-TOMORROW-AND-WOULD-YOU-JUST-DIE-ALREADY"?
REAARRGHH!

SKREEEEEEE...
HCK*

YOU WANT TO TAKE CARE OF NEEDLE-FACE?

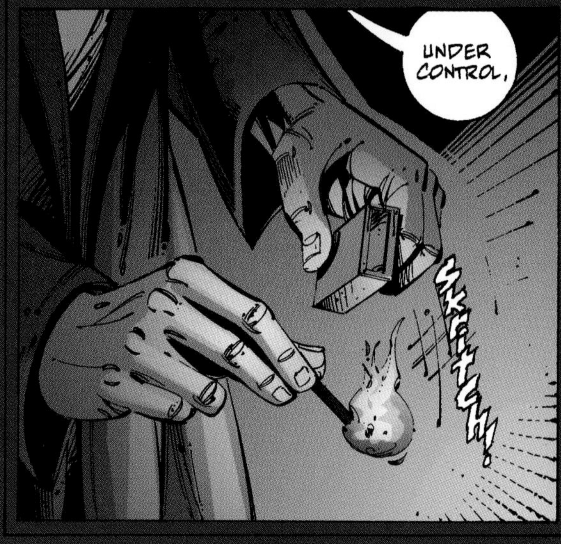
UNDER CONTROL.
SKRITCH!

WOULDN'T WANT THE CARETAKER FINDING THIS MESS IN THE MORNING. DON'T KNOW HOW THE COPS WOULD EXPLAIN THAT ONE AWAY.
FWOOOSH

THEY'D FIND A WAY. THEY ALWAYS DO.
SO, ARE YOU READY FOR THAT TEST TOMORROW?
I'LL BE ALL RIGHT...

...AS LONG AS NOTHING ELSE COMES UP.

Sunnydale High School.
Unlikely as it may seem, the strategies in the war against darkness are planned within these walls.
For each Slayer, there is a Watcher. A scholar learned in the mysteries of chaos, skilled in the ways of the warrior, assigned the venerable duty of training the Slayer.

And, since Buffy Summmers insists on remaining a student, her Watcher, Rupert Giles, has found a way to stay close to her, and to his vast collection of arcane tomes.
They've got quite a library at Sunnydale High. And quite a librarian.
AH, HERE WE ARE, THEN, EXCELLENT.

...PLEASE ANGEL, OF COURSE HE'S STILL HERE I MEAN, HE'S GILES.

GILES? HIDEY-HO, NEIGHBOR, YOU ARE STILL HERE, RIGHT?

OF COURSE I'M STILL HERE, BUFFY. AFTER ALL, WHERE ELSE WOULD I GO?

I'M GILES.

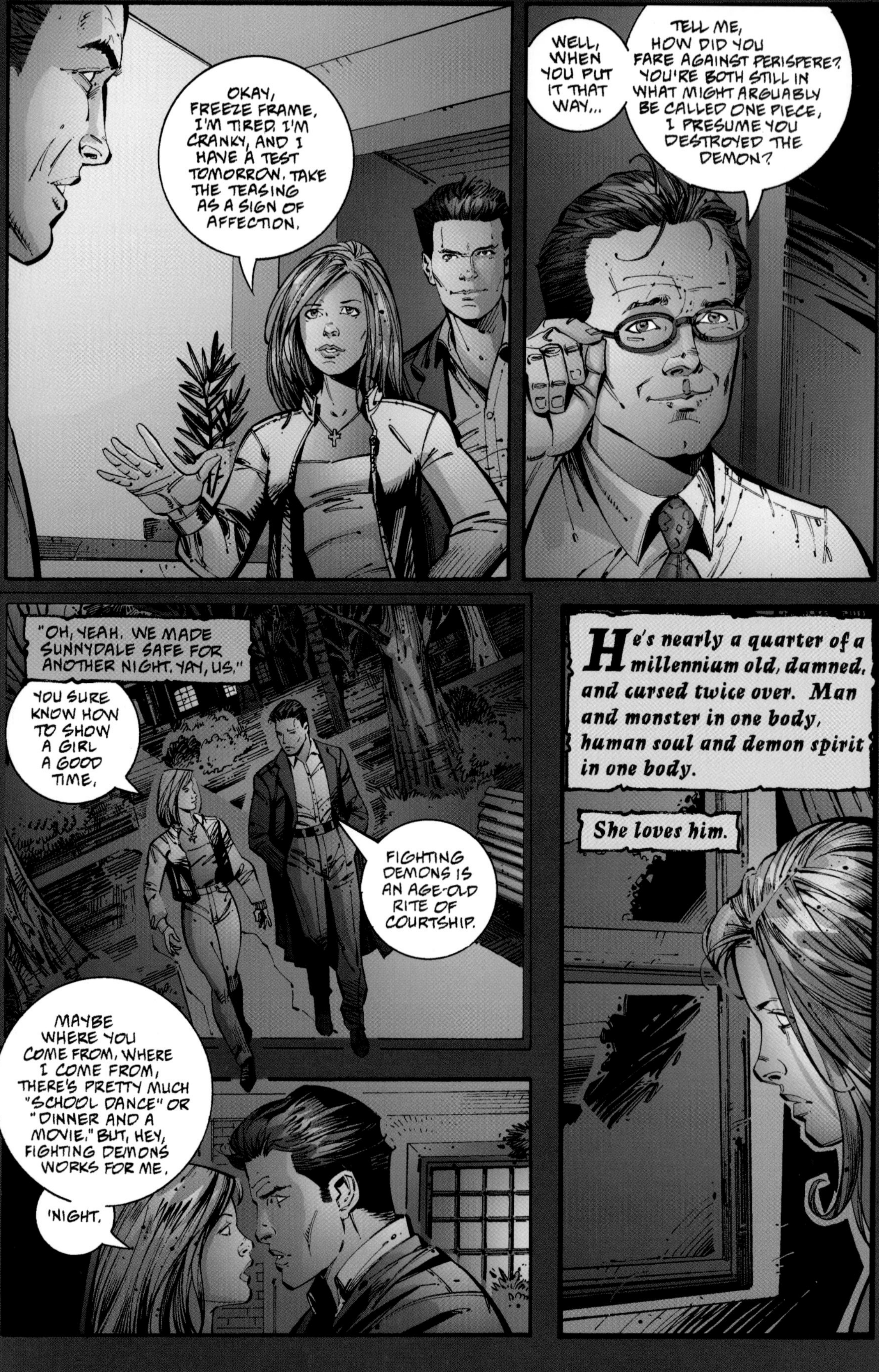

OKAY, FREEZE FRAME. I'M TIRED. I'M CRANKY, AND I HAVE A TEST TOMORROW. TAKE THE TEASING AS A SIGN OF AFFECTION.

WELL, WHEN YOU PUT IT THAT WAY...

TELL ME, HOW DID YOU FARE AGAINST PERISPERE? YOU'RE BOTH STILL IN WHAT MIGHT ARGUABLY BE CALLED ONE PIECE. I PRESUME YOU DESTROYED THE DEMON?

"OH, YEAH. WE MADE SUNNYDALE SAFE FOR ANOTHER NIGHT. YAY, US."
YOU SURE KNOW HOW TO SHOW A GIRL A GOOD TIME.
FIGHTING DEMONS IS AN AGE-OLD RITE OF COURTSHIP.
MAYBE WHERE YOU COME FROM. WHERE I COME FROM, THERE'S PRETTY MUCH "SCHOOL DANCE" OR "DINNER AND A MOVIE." BUT, HEY, FIGHTING DEMONS WORKS FOR ME.
'NIGHT.

He's nearly a quarter of a millennium old, damned, and cursed twice over. Man and monster in one body, human soul and demon spirit in one body.
She loves him.

She's so young. A girl. But a girl chosen, destined to live her life for a greater purpose. Cursed, in some ways, just as he is. She should kill him.
He loves her.
he feeling is so strong between them, that each ignores the certainty in their hearts, the know-ledge that it can never work.
heir love is doomed, and yet, they go on.
It makes them both a bit... irritable, at times.
ANGELUS.
NO, NO. DON'T SAY IT. THREATS, BRAGGING. I HEAR IT ALL THE TIME. JUST KEEP QUIET. BRING IT ON, AND DIE.
WE HAVEN'T COME TO DIE, ANGEL. BELIEVE IT OR NOT, WE'VE COME TO TALK.
CATHERINE?

Vienna, Austria-Hungary, 1892.
A city of beauty and prosperity, where the Old World is in every stone of every structure ...but its citizens can taste the new century just around the corner.
Vienna is a cosmopolitan city. Its people have no time for their Old World beginnings, or the accompanying superstition.
But that doesn't mean it isn't there.
ALL RIGHT, YER BLOODY HIGHNESS, WE'RE HERE.
NEXT TIME, THOUGH, YOU DRIVE.
THAT'S A DEAL, M'LAD. NOW COME ON UP HERE. I SAVED YOU THE BEST OF THE LOT. A PLUMP LITTLE TART SHE IS, RIPE FOR THE PICKING.

COME HERE, DEAR. SPIKE WON'T HURT YOU. NOT FOR VERY LONG, AT LEAST.
REALLY VERY KIND OF YOU, ANGEL. VERY KIND, INDEED. SURE YOU WON'T HAVE A NIP?

YOU GO AHEAD, DEAR WILLIAM. I'LL JUST WATCH.

DON'T MIND IF I DO.

AIEEEEE
HA HA HA, GOOD SHOW, SPIKE, LOOK AT HER SQUIRM.
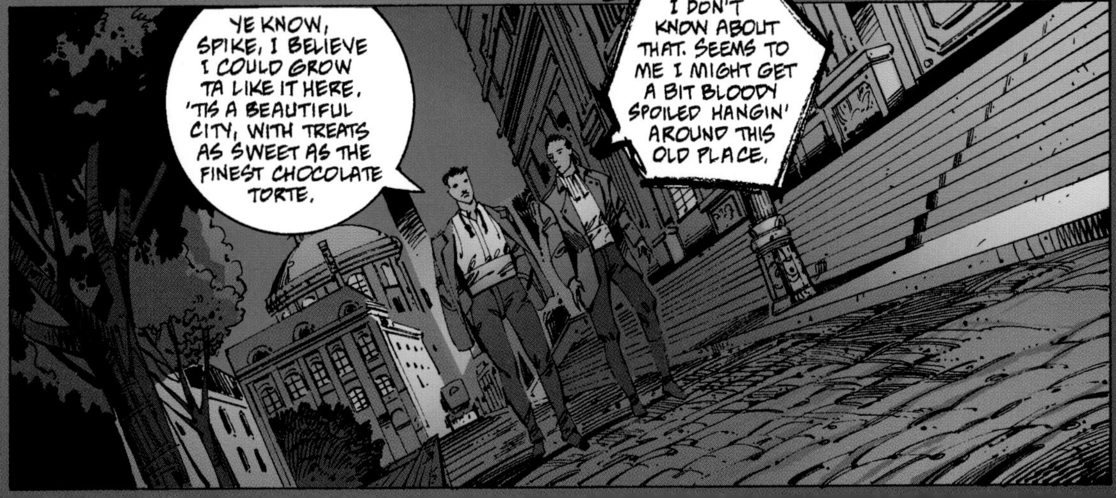
YE KNOW, SPIKE, I BELIEVE I COULD GROW TA LIKE IT HERE. 'TIS A BEAUTIFUL CITY, WITH TREATS AS SWEET AS THE FINEST CHOCOLATE TORTE.
I DON'T KNOW ABOUT THAT. SEEMS TO ME I MIGHT GET A BIT BLOODY SPOILED HANGIN' AROUND THIS OLD PLACE.

WHAT'S WRONG WITH BEING A BIT SPOILED, THEN, EH? I'M QUITE USED TO GETTING WHAT I WANT, LAD. YOU'LL GROW USED TO IT AS WELL.
FOR MY PART, I'M GRATEFUL DRUSILLA CONVINCED US TO VISIT VIENNA.
INDEED. IT'S OUR KIND OF TOWN. EVERYONE'S TOO BLOODY SOPHISTICATED TO BELIEVE IN VAMPIRES. RIGHT UP UNTIL WE RIP THEIR THROATS OUT.
OH, BOYS, THERE YOU ARE. THE WINDOWS WHISPERED TO ME, AND I DIDN'T BELIEVE THEM. BUT HERE YOU ARE JUST THE SAME. COME UP NOW. OH, YOU MUST, FOR I HAVE A LITTLE SURPRISE WAITING...
ARE YE THINKIN' WHAT I'M THINKIN'?
I WAS JUST RECALLING THE LAST TIME DRUSILLA SAID SHE HAD A SURPRISE FOR YOU.
AYE, LAD. MY THOUGHT AS WELL. I STILL HAVE SCARS FROM THAT NIGHT.
ALL RIGHT, DRU, LET'S HAVE YOUR SURPRISE, THEN...
HER NAME IS CATHERINE. SHE'S FOR YOU, ANGEL. ALL FOR YOU.

TAKE HIM!
I THOUGHT YOU SAID YOU JUST WANTED TO TALK.
I WANT TO MAKE ABSOLUTELY CERTAIN YOU'RE GOING TO LISTEN.
DON'T STRUGGLE, ANGELUS. WE'RE NOT GOING TO KILL YOU.
DAMN RIGHT YOU'RE NOT! I MAY BE FOOL ENOUGH TO GIVE YOU THE BENEFIT OF THE DOUBT, BUT IF YOU WANT A FIGHT--
I'LL GIVE YOU ONE!

ALL RIGHT, THAT'S ENOUGH. GET AWAY FROM HIM! I CAN'T AFFORD TO LOSE YOU ALL BEFORE THE BATTLE EVEN BEGINS.
HE'S KILLED GAVIN, CATH! HE'LL DIE FOR THAT!
SO, THIS IS YOUR IDEA OF THE ART OF CONVERSATION, CATHERINE? I TAUGHT YOU TOO WELL, I SUPPOSE.
ANGEL, NO! I... I SHOULDN'T'VE DONE IT THIS WAY. I JUST DIDN'T THINK YOU'D LISTEN. BUT YOU HAVE TO. PLEASE, THIRTY SECONDS. THAT'S ALL I ASK. FOR OLD TIMES' SAKE.
FOR OLD TIMES' SAKE? YOU'RE KIDDING, RIGHT? I SPEND EVERY WAKING MOMENT TRYING TO MAKE UP FOR WHAT I DID IN THOSE "OLD TIMES."
LOOK, I WENT ABOUT THIS WRONG. IF YOU HAVE TO KILL ME, YOU KILL ME. BUT JUST LISTEN, PLEASE. JUST FOR A FEW SECONDS.
I NEED YOUR HELP, ANGEL. WE ALL DO.
IT'S THE HOLLOWER.

JUST STAY BY MY SIDE, LASS. ANGEL WILL TEACH YE ALL YE NEED T'KNOW OF HUNTIN' HUMANS.
"WHAT YE HAVE TO UNDERSTAND, LOVE, IS THE FLAVORS. THERE ARE SO MANY DIFFERENT KINDS. SOMETIMES THE SLIGHTEST WEE THING CAN MAKE ALL THE DIFFERENCE.
"IF THEY SUFFER FIRST, THAT'S BEST. AYE, AND TERROR ADDS SPICE TO THE BLOOD, LIKE NOTHING YE'VE EVER TASTED."
NOW, LASS, THE TIME HAS COME. YE'RE GOING TO JUST LOVE THIS PART.
knock knock knock

<PLEASE, SIR, LET ME IN. HE'S BEEN AT ME, SIR. I STRUCK HIM AND RAN, BUT I THINK... I THINK HE'S STILL OUT THERE>*
* TRANSLATED FROM THE GERMAN--ED.
<COME IN, MISS. COME IN. YOU SAY HE'S STILL OUT THERE? I HOPE YOU'RE RIGHT. I'LL GIVE HIM A LESSON IN HOW TO TREAT A LADY.>
OH, ANGEL, LOVE, YOU WERE SO RIGHT. IT WAS SO PERFECT. AND THE LOOK IN THE GIRL'S EYES... SHE WAS THE SWEETEST, RICHEST THING I'VE EVER TASTED.
THAT'S WHY I LOVE THIS TOWN, LASS. SO MANY FLAVORS! WHAT SHALL WE TASTE NEXT, THEN?
WHAT ABOUT HIM?

OH, YES, ANGEL. I THINK HE'LL DO JUST FINE.

<NOW! TAKE HIM, OR WE STARVE!>
<N-N-NO! GET BACK!>

YOU HEARD HIM, YOU WITHERED BEASTS! GET BACK! THE BOY IS OUR PREY, NOT FOR THE LIKES OF YOU!

ANGEL, NO!
< INTERFERE, AND YOU'LL DIE WITH HIM! WE'RE TOO HUNGRY TO FEAR YOU. WE FEED TONIGHT, OR WE DIE! >

THEN DIE.

<YOU AWFUL, GLUTTONOUS WENCH! YOU'VE ALREADY FED TONIGHT! I SMELL IT ON YOU! AND YOU'D DENY US THIS BOY?>
<SURVIVAL OF THE FITTEST, MAGGOT, WHICH YOU, CLEARLY ARE NOT. I'VE NEVER SEEN SUCH A PITIFUL-->
<NEVER SEEN? NEVER SEEN? BUT SOON, YOU'LL BE JUST LIKE US, HIDING IN THE SHADOWS, TOO AFRAID EVEN TO HUNT, UNTIL THE BLOODLUST GETS SO STRONG THAT-->
<NO. I'M NOT GOING TO TELL YOU. YOU'LL MEET THE HOLLOWER SOON ENOUGH.
YOU'LL GET WHAT YOU DESERVE.
GO THEN. YE'VE ALREADY LOST US OUR MEAL. YE'RE NOT WORTH THE CHASE.
ARE YOU ALL RIGHT, THEN?
I'LL BE FINE, YES. BUT WHAT WAS ALL THAT? WHAT IS THE HOLLOWER?
I WISH I KNEW.

LIAR!
WE DESTROYED THE HOLLOWER, CATHERINE. DON'T YOU REMEMBER? YOU, ME, SPIKE, AND DRUSILLA. IT'S DEAD.
YOU WERE NEVER THIS MUCH OF A FOOL BEFORE YOU GOT YOUR SOUL BACK, ANGEL.
SOMETHING THAT POWERFUL ISN'T SO EASY TO KILL.

I DON'T CARE, DON'T YOU SEE?
IF THE HOLLOWER'S BACK, ALL THE BETTER.
OTHER THAN THE SLAYER, IT'S THE ONLY NATURAL PREDATOR VAMPIRES HAVE. WHY IN HELL WOULD I WANT TO HELP YOU?

CATHERINE, WHAT ARE YOU--
BACK OFF. IT'S UP TO HIM NOW.
ALL RIGHT. YOU'VE BOUGHT YOURSELF THIRTY SECONDS.
FORGET THIRTY SECONDS. I NEED YOU TO LISTEN TO ME.
YOU WANT TO KILL ME SO BADLY...
...THEN KILL ME.
BUT IF YOU KILL ME, YOU WON'T EVEN HAVE ANY WARNING, AND THE HOLOCAUST WILL BE UPON YOU.

FINE, TALK THEN. NO THREATS. NO PROMISES.
"I'M SURE YOUR LITTLE GIRLFRIEND HAS NOTICED IT BY NOW. NO VAMPIRES. OR AT LEAST, VERY FEW.
"THEY'RE NOT HUNTING. THEY'RE NOT HIDING. THEY'RE EITHER DEAD, OR THEY'VE LEFT TOWN.
"A SLAYER'S WET DREAM, RIGHT?
"BUT YOU'RE MISSING SOME-THING IMPORTANT. SEE, I'VE DONE SOME RESEARCH ON THE HOLLOWER.
"SURE, IT'S HUNTING US. HUNTING YOU, TOO, LET'S NOT FORGET. MAYBE YOU WON'T KILL IT TO SAVE US, OR EVEN TO SAVE YOURSELF."
BUT I'M WILLING TO BET YOU'D DO WHATEVER YOU HAVE TO DO...
TO STOP MOST OF THIS TOWN FROM BECOMING VAMPIRES IN A SINGLE NIGHT.
UNLESS WE KILL IT FIRST.

At first glance, Sunnydale is an idyllic little place, fitting the image of perfection and carefree bliss that Southern California has become in the national myth.
But Sunnydale isn't any of those things--it's the dark, twisted funhouse reflection of that image.
Here, nothing is what it seems. Vampires stalk the night, forcing the locals to realize they are no longer on top of the food chain.
But then...
...neither are the vampires.
"... SO, I'M SITTING THERE, BARELY ABLE TO SIT UP FROM LOSING SO MUCH BLOOD, THINKING 'THIS THING WITH THE FREAKIN' TENTACLES IS COMING BACK FOR SECONDS SOON'..."

...AND, Y'KNOW, I'D BETTER GET OUT OF THERE. BUT IT'S, LIKE, FIVE MINUTES BEFORE I CAN EVEN STAND UP. AND THE WEIRDEST THING IS...
...THE THING NEVER COMES BACK.
UH-HUH. SO, WHY WERE YOU REALLY OUT OF SCHOOL YESTERDAY?

DUDE, I TOLD YOU YOU WOULDN'T BELIEVE ME! WHY DON'T YOU GO UP THERE AND HAVE A LOOK? WE'LL SEE IF YOU MAKE IT BACK.
I'LL GO. ABSOLUTELY. MAYBE I CAN GET MAGGIE TO COME WITH ME. SHE'LL BE ALL TERRIFIED AND SNUGGLY.

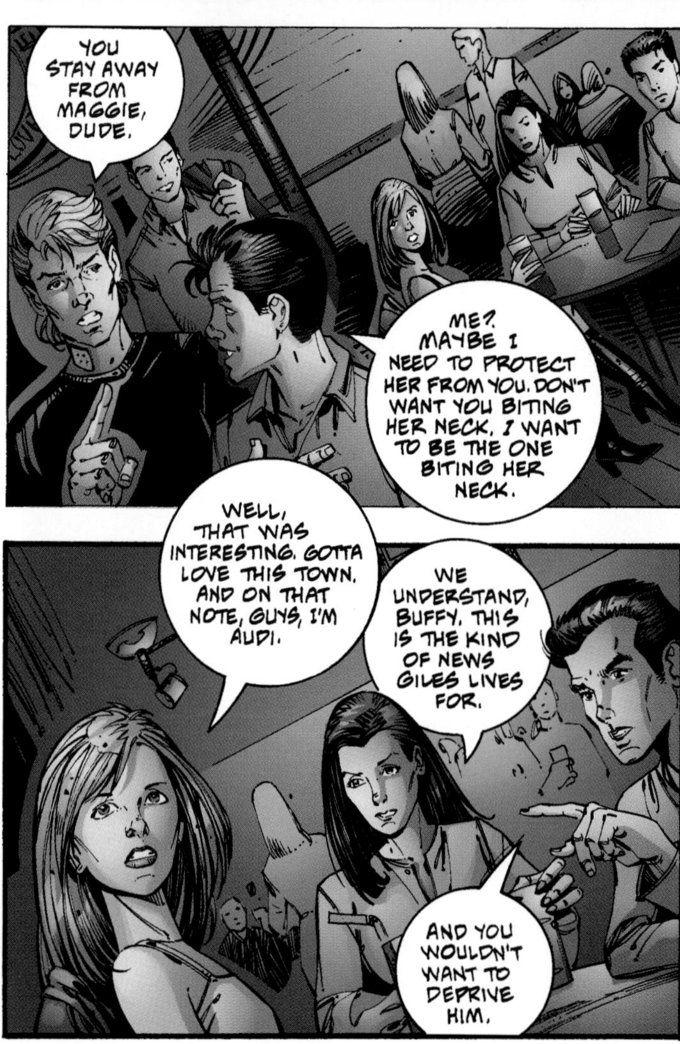
YOU STAY AWAY FROM MAGGIE, DUDE.
ME? MAYBE I NEED TO PROTECT HER FROM YOU. DON'T WANT YOU BITING HER NECK. I WANT TO BE THE ONE BITING HER NECK.
WELL, THAT WAS INTERESTING. GOTTA LOVE THIS TOWN. AND ON THAT NOTE, GUYS, I'M AUDI.
WE UNDERSTAND, BUFFY. THIS IS THE KIND OF NEWS GILES LIVES FOR.
AND YOU WOULDN'T WANT TO DEPRIVE HIM.

GREAT. WHAT IS IT THIS TIME?

NOTHING. I'VE ONLY EVER SEEN REFERENCES TO THE HOLLOWER IN ONE BOOK, AND I LOST THAT AGES AGO. EVEN THEN, WE COULDN'T DO MUCH MORE THAN HURT IT.

BUT IF WE CAN HURT IT ENOUGH, MAYBE WE CAN GET CLOSE ENOUGH TO KILL IT. THE ALTERNATIVE IS UNTHINKABLE FOR BOTH OF US.
YOU'VE GOT TO FIND SOMETHING, ANGELUS.

STOP CALLING ME THAT! YOU NEVER CALLED ME THAT, NOT EVEN WHEN WE WERE... TOGETHER.
JUST TRYING TO REMIND YOU WHO YOU ARE.

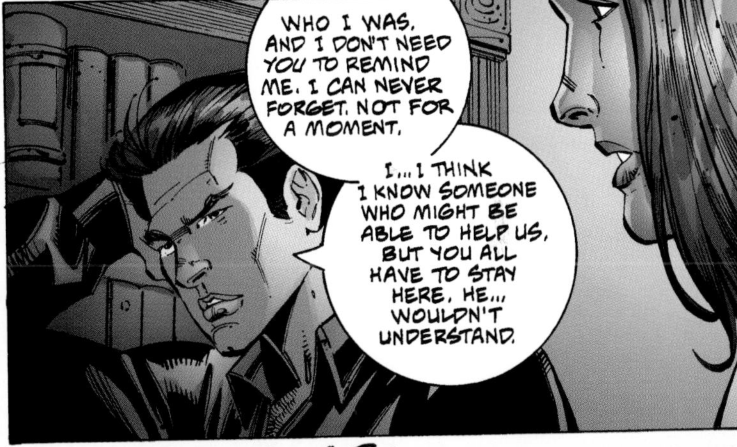
WHO I WAS. AND I DON'T NEED YOU TO REMIND ME. I CAN NEVER FORGET. NOT FOR A MOMENT.
I... I THINK I KNOW SOMEONE WHO MIGHT BE ABLE TO HELP US. BUT YOU ALL HAVE TO STAY HERE. HE... WOULDN'T UNDERSTAND.

RING! RING!
EXPECTING ANYONE?
NO.

RING!

BUFFY, HEY.
HEY, LOOKS LIKE WE'VE GOT A BIG NEW EVIL REARING ITS SLIMY TENTACLED HEAD.
I'M ON MY WAY TO SEE GILES, THEN OUT ON PATROL. WANNA COME?

YOU CAN JUST FINISH WHATEVER YOU'RE DOING, AND THEN WE'LL... ANGEL?
NOW'S NOT A GOOD TIME, BUFFY.

ANGEL?

HE SHUT YOU OUT?
LIKE I WAS A JEHOVAH'S WITNESS. COULDN'T CLOSE THE DOOR FAST ENOUGH. WITH THE WHOLE MODELING THING...
...I HAVEN'T SEEN HIM MUCH LATELY, AND I JUST... DON'T YOU THINK IT'S WEIRD?
Hmmm. OH, YES. QUITE. COULD YOU TELL ME ABOUT THE "TENTACLED THING" AGAIN?

Vienna, Austria-Hungary, 1892.
AIEEEEEEEEE

<GOD, NO, PLEASE! LORD, SAVE ME!>

<I... I'LL GIVE MY LIFE TO THE CHURCH, LORD. I SWEAR. JUST, PLEASE...>

<OH, DON'T EVEN SAY THAT, LOVE. THAT'D BE A BLOODY SHAME, SWEET GIRL LIKE YOU.>

WOULDN'T IT, DRU?

OH, YES. I CAN THINK OF SO MANY MORE... ARTISTIC WAYS TO USE YOU. I CAN HEAR YOUR BLOOD SING.

<NO, PLEASE... PLEASE DON'T TOUCH ME...>

IT'S A WONDERFUL PARTY, ANGELUS. YOU SHOULD BE PROUD. I NEVER IMAGINED VAMPIRES COULD BE SO SOCIABLE.
HISTORICALLY, OUR KIND DO TEND MORE TOWARD SQUABBLIN' THAN CELEBRATION. BUT I'VE ALWAYS BEEN MORE OF A LOVER THAN A FIGHTER, MY DEAR.
AND, I HAVE TO CONFESS, LASS, IT DOES ME COLD HEART GOOD TO SEE EVERYONE HAVIN' SUCH A WONDERFUL TIME.
YE SURE KNOW HOW TO THROW A PARTY, ANGEL. IT'S LIKE BLOODY CHRISTMAS, IT IS.
IT IS A LOVELY PARTY, THOUGH IT DOESN'T SEEM QUITE RIGHT WITHOUT TEA AND CAKES.
THANK YE BOTH. OUR KIND SPENDS SO MUCH TIME PLANNIN' FOR THE DAY WHEN THE BLOOD FLOWS LIKE WINE...
...WHEN, PERSONALLY, I'VE NEVER UNDERSTOOD WHAT WE'RE WAITIN' FOR.

SPEAKING OF WINE, ANGELUS, I THINK IT'S TIME WE BROUGHT ANOTHER "DECANTER" UP FROM THE CELLAR. LAST I SAW, THERE WAS STILL A YOUNG LADY DOWN THERE WHO LOOKED PARTICULARLY RIPE.
TIME FOR A TASTE, DON'T YOU.. AARRRGH!
WHAT IN HELL IS THAT?!
I THINK IT'S RATHER PRETTY. CAN I KEEP IT?
WHEREVER THIS THING CAME FROM, DRUSILLA, IT ISN'T GOING TO BE YOUR HOUSE PET.

ANGELUS, HELP ME, I...
KARL! DAMNED THING... WHY IS IT ATTACKING US, INSTEAD OF THE HUMANS?
IT HAS A TASTE FOR VAMPIRES, LOVE...

"...IT'S DRAINING SOMETHING OUT OF HIM."

THAT'LL BE ENOUGH OF THAT!

POOR KARL, JUST LIE STILL AND WE'LL... OH, SPIKE, HELP ME! SO COLD INSIDE. I CAN FEEL IT. HE'S EMPTY AS A CHURCH COFFER--THE DEMON'S BEEN SUCKED RIGHT OUT!

THAT'S IMPOSSIBLE, DRU. THE DEMON INSIDE IS THE ONLY THING KEEPING A VAMPIRE ALIVE, WITHOUT IT...
RIGHT, THEN. NEVER MIND.

CATHERINE, NO!

SORRY, OLD BOY, BUT I'M GOING TO HAVE TO TAKE BACK WHAT I SAID ABOUT YOUR PARTY. A BLOODY DISASTER, WASN'T IT?
ANGEL, REMEMBER THAT RAGGED VAMPIRE WE MET LAST WEEK? WHAT WAS IT HE WAS BABBLING ABOUT? THE HOLLOWER, I THINK HE SAID. DO YOU SUPPOSE HE MEANT THAT THING?
WHATEVER IT IS, LASS, WE'RE GOIN' TA KILL IT.

OKAY, GILES, I'M ALL FOR BEING PREPARED AND ALL, BUT HAVE YOU EVER EVEN HEARD THE WORD "OVERKILL"?
PLEASE, BUFFY, I'M GOING TO BEGIN MY RESEARCH RIGHT AWAY, BUT UNTIL WE CAN DETERMINE PRECISELY WHAT IT IS YOU'LL BE FACING...
...YOU'D BEST BE READY FOR ANYTHING.
I'M TEMPTED TO SAY "I WAS BORN READY," BUT I'M NOT SURE I COULD'VE WORKED A CROSSBOW AS AN INFANT.

Y'KNOW, THOUGH, I THINK I LIKE THE WHOLE SHOULDER-HARNESS THING.
IT ISN'T ANYWHERE NEAR THE FASHION IMPEDIMENT I EXPECTED IT TO BE.
WHAT? OH, YES, WELL, DO BE CAREFUL, BUFFY.
YEAH, YOU, TOO. WATCH OUT FOR DEMONIC PAPER CUTS.

CHECK IN SHORTLY, WILL YOU? PERHAPS I'LL HAVE SOMETHING FOR YOU THEN.
KREEEAK
Hmmm. BACK SO SOON?

BUFFY, DID YOU FORGET--?
NOT QUITE.

OH, ANGEL. IT'S YOU. I'M AFRAID YOU'VE JUST MISSED BUFFY.
I DIDN'T COME TO SEE BUFFY. I CAME TO SEE YOU.

BUFFY MENTIONED YOU'D BEEN BEHAVING ODDLY. WHAT IS IT THAT'S TROUBLING YOU? I HOPE YOU HAVEN'T BEEN HAVING A PROBLEM WITH... SELF-CONTROL.

I'M FINE. HAVE YOU EVER HEARD OF THE HOLLOWER?

THE HOLLOWER, OF COURSE! IT MUST BE WHAT KILLED THE VAMPIRE THAT ATTACKED THE HATCHER BOY. I RECALL READING ABOUT IT, BUT I'M NOT SURE WHICH VOLUME.

OF COURSE, IF THE CREATURE TRULY DOES EXIST, I'M NOT SURE WHY WE WOULD WANT TO STOP IT.
I'VE FACED IT BEFORE. AND I WOULD HAVE AGREED WITH YOU, BUT IF WHAT I'VE BEEN TOLD IS TRUE--

AH, HERE IT IS, *CRAWLING BEASTS*, BY DEMETRIUS. I BELIEVE I EVEN MARKED THE PAGE, THOUGH I DIDN'T READ THE ENTIRE PASSAGE.

NOW LET'S SEE... OH. OH, DEAR. I HADN'T READ THIS FAR LISTEN TO THIS--
"ACCORDING TO ALL ACCEPTED DEMON LORE, THE HOLLOWER MAY CONSUME ONLY THREE THOUSAND DEMON SOULS FROM ITS VAMPIRIC VICTIMS BEFORE IT CANNOT CONTAIN THEM ANY LONGER.
"AT WHICH TIME, IT REGURGITATES ALL THOSE DEMONS, IN A SPIRIT FORM WITH WHICH THEY CAN INHABIT AND TRANS-FORM LIVING HUMAN BEINGS, NOT JUST CORPSES, INTO VAMPIRES.
THIS HAS HAPPENED AT LEAST TWICE IN ANCIENT TIMES, BUT THERE IS NO RECORD OF A MODERN EQUIVALENT."
DEAR GOD. THREE THOUSAND PEOPLE IN SUNNYDALE TRANSFORMED INTO VAMPIRES IN AN INSTANT. IT WOULD BE A VAMPIRE HOLOCAUST. WE'VE GOT TO STOP IT.
NOT WE, GILES.
I TRIED TO KILL IT ONCE BEFORE, AND FAILED. BUFFY HAS OTHER THINGS TO WORRY ABOUT. I CAME TO TELL YOU TO KEEP HER AWAY. I'LL TAKE CARE OF THE HOLLOWER.
ANGEL, WAIT...
BUFFY'S ALREADY OUT LOOKING FOR IT.

IT WAS HERE ALL RIGHT, BUT WITH THE SEA BREEZE, I'VE LOST THE SCENT.
CATHERINE WON'T BE PLEASED. IF WE CAN'T TRACK THE THING, ANGELUS CAN'T KILL IT.
I'M NOT SURE ANGELUS CAN KILL IT ANYWAY. BUT I SUPPOSE WE'LL SEE.
THROUGH HERE. I THINK I'VE GOT THE SCENT AGAIN, GROWING STRONGER NOW.
YOU'VE BEEN SAYING THAT ALL NIGHT.
I CAN'T WAIT TO FIND OUT WHAT *THAT* WAS ALL ABOUT.

COME ON, MUFFIN, MOVE ALONG, DEAR. WE HAVEN'T ALL NIGHT, YOU KNOW.
THAT'S ONE WAY TO PUT IT!
ABOUT TIME WE TOOK A LUNCH BREAK. I THOUGHT I WAS GONNA STARVE.
YOU WERE RIGHT!
GET AWAY FROM ME, YOU...YOU PUNKS!
OR HERE'S ANOTHER IDEA, MISTER--
--YOU COULD RUN!
YIP YIP
THAT'S IT, MUFFIN, RUN!
WELL, WHAT HAVE WE HERE? THE SLAYER, ARE YOU? WE'VE HEARD ABOUT YOU.
FAME, DOESN'T IT SUCK?

DID THIS "CATHERINE" GIVE YOU ANY INSTRUCTIONS ABOUT *NOT GETTING* KILLED? THAT WOULD HAVE COME IN KIND OF HANDY RIGHT ABOUT-- OWWW!
YOU LOOK TASTY, SLAYER, AND CATHERINE DIDN'T SAY A WORD ABOUT NOT KILLING YOU.
YOU UNDERESTIMATE US, SLAYER. WE WERE SIRED BY THE MISTRESS HERSELF, CATHERINE DeLANCIE. WE WON'T BE KILLED SO EASILY.
WHAT? NO, NOT NOW!
AIIEEEEEE
WHAT WAS THAT YOU WERE SAYING?
YOU LITTLE-- YOU'VE KILLED HIM NOW, DAMN YOU. THE HOLLOWER'S GOT HIM.
AIIEEEEEE

YEAH, MY HEART... BLEEDS... OH, BOY... NICE DEMON, NICE DEMON...
BIG UGLY DEMON, WHO'S APPARENTLY MORE INTERESTED IN KILLING VAMPIRES THAN LITTLE OLD ME.
MAYBE I'LL JUST TRY TO FIGURE OUT WHAT I'M UP AGAINST BEFORE I--
HEY, WHERE DO YOU THINK YOU'RE GOING?
YOU HUNT US WHEN YOU SHOULD BE THANKING US, SLAYER! IF NOT FOR OUR MISTRESS, ANGEL WOULD NOT HAVE A CHANCE TO SAVE THIS PLACE.
ANGEL? WAIT A MINUTE, WHAT DOES ANY OF THIS HAVE TO DO WITH--
--ANGEL? AND, WOW, HE'S FAST. NOW THE FLASH IS A VAMPIRE. GREAT.

YOO HOO, ANYBODY --WHOA.
RISE AND SHINE, SPANKY.
YOU CAN'T BE DEAD. IF YOU WERE DEAD, YOU'D BE--
--DUST? WELL, THAT WAS NEW.
LOOKS LIKE DEATH BY HOLLOWER IS A WHOLE NEW EXPERIENCE.
AND SPEAKING OF SLIME-BOY... HOW DO YOU MAKE A TWO-TON ELDER DEMON DISAPPEAR?
THIS CAN'T BE GOOD.

1892.
WE'RE ALL AGREED THEN. THE HOLLOWER MUST DIE.
I'VE FOUND LITTLE REFERENCE TO IT, BUT I DID FIND SOMETHING. NOT MUCH MORE THAN A LITTLE CHARM, REALLY, BUT IT OUGHT TO LET US GET IN CLOSE.
AND IF WE CAN GET CLOSE ENOUGH, WE CAN KILL IT. AND IF WE DON'T...
THIS BEASTIE FEEDS ON THE DEMONS INSIDE US. WE EITHER KILL IT, OR ONE DAY, WE'LL ALL END UP ON ITS DINNER PLATE.
NOW, THEN, ARE YE WITH ME?
WE'RE WITH YOU, ANGELUS.

STAY CLOSE, WE DON'T WANT IT THINNING OUR RANKS BEFORE WE EVEN REACH THE INFERNAL THING.
BACK INSIDE, YE FOOL, NOTHING FOR YOU TO SEE HERE.
COME ON THEN, MY LADS, THE DEMON GIVES OFF A POWERFUL BLOOD SCENT.
YE'RE THE BEST TRACKERS WE'VE GOT. FIND THE HOLLOWER FOR US.
WELL DONE, LADS! YE'VE FOUND ITS BOLT-HOLE!
NOW WE'LL SEND THE HOLLOWER BACK TO HELL ON AN EMPTY STOMACH.

MUST BE A REAL PAGE-TURNER,
WHO THE DEVIL,..
...AHHH,..
BUFFY, I'VE TOLD YOU NOT TO SNEAK UP ON ME LIKE THAT. I'VE SPILLED MY TEA,
SORRY ABOUT THE TEA, AND THE SHIRT. BUT I THINK WE HAVE BIGGER PROBLEMS AT THE PRESENT.
THE HOLLOWER?. YES, I KNOW, ANGEL WAS BY. IF WE CAN'T DESTROY THIS DEMON, THE RESULTS COULD BE CATACLYSMIC. IN FACT, I'VE BEEN READING UP ON POSSIBLE--
YOU KNOW?. WELL, THANKS FOR SHARING,
PLEASE, BUFFY, I'VE ONLY JUST FOUND OUT MYSELF, LET'S CALM DOWN, SHALL WE, SO THAT WE CAN DETERMINE HOW BEST TO COMBAT THE HOLLOWER?
PERHAPS YOU'D LIKE SOME TEA?
TEA! THAT'S YOUR ANSWER TO EVERY-THING!

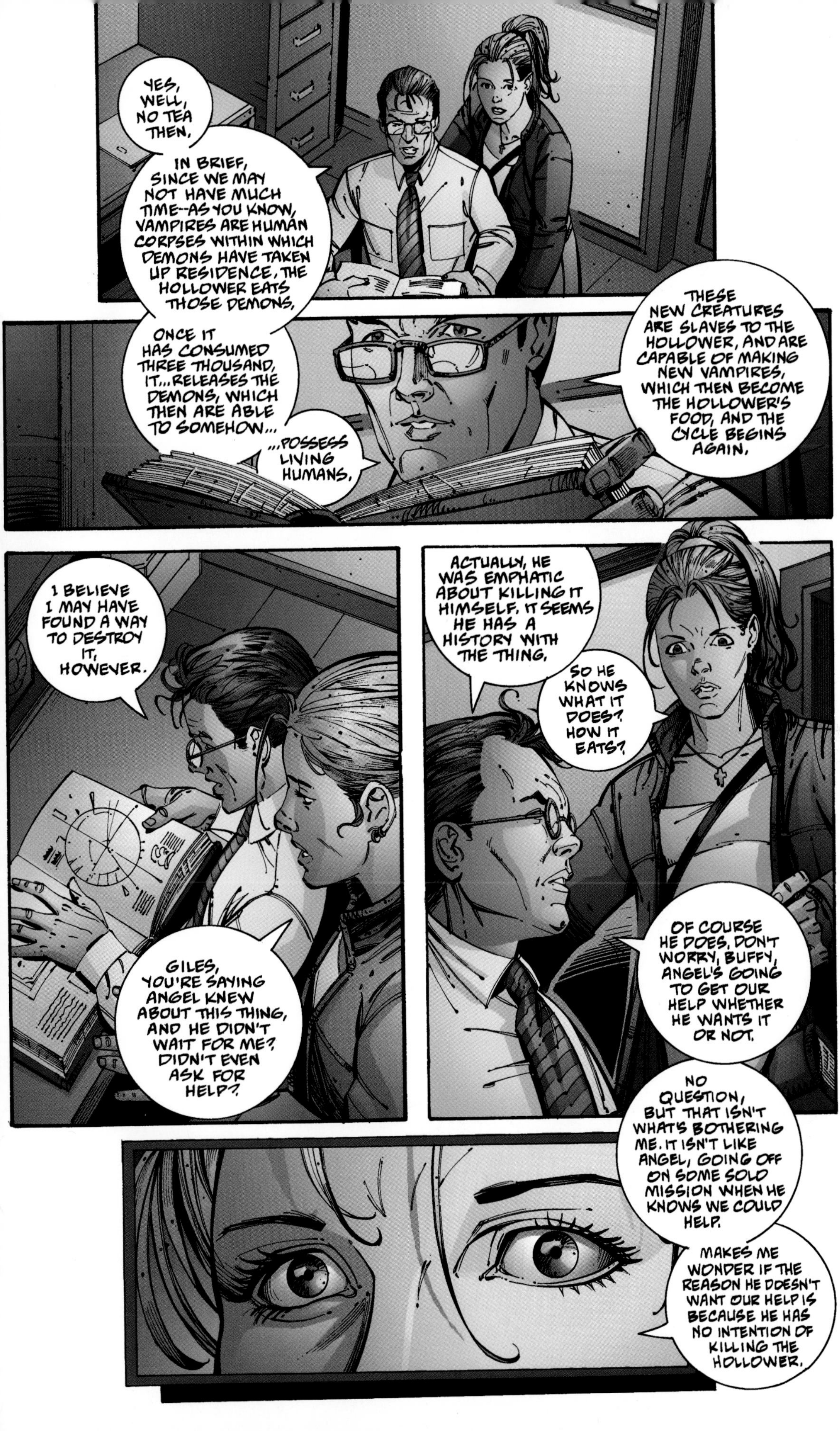

YES, WELL, NO TEA THEN.

IN BRIEF, SINCE WE MAY NOT HAVE MUCH TIME--AS YOU KNOW, VAMPIRES ARE HUMAN CORPSES WITHIN WHICH DEMONS HAVE TAKEN UP RESIDENCE. THE HOLLOWER EATS THOSE DEMONS.

ONCE IT HAS CONSUMED THREE THOUSAND, IT... RELEASES THE DEMONS, WHICH THEN ARE ABLE TO SOMEHOW...

...POSSESS LIVING HUMANS.

THESE NEW CREATURES ARE SLAVES TO THE HOLLOWER, AND ARE CAPABLE OF MAKING NEW VAMPIRES, WHICH THEN BECOME THE HOLLOWER'S FOOD, AND THE CYCLE BEGINS AGAIN.

I BELIEVE I MAY HAVE FOUND A WAY TO DESTROY IT, HOWEVER.
GILES, YOU'RE SAYING ANGEL KNEW ABOUT THIS THING, AND HE DIDN'T WAIT FOR ME? DIDN'T EVEN ASK FOR HELP?

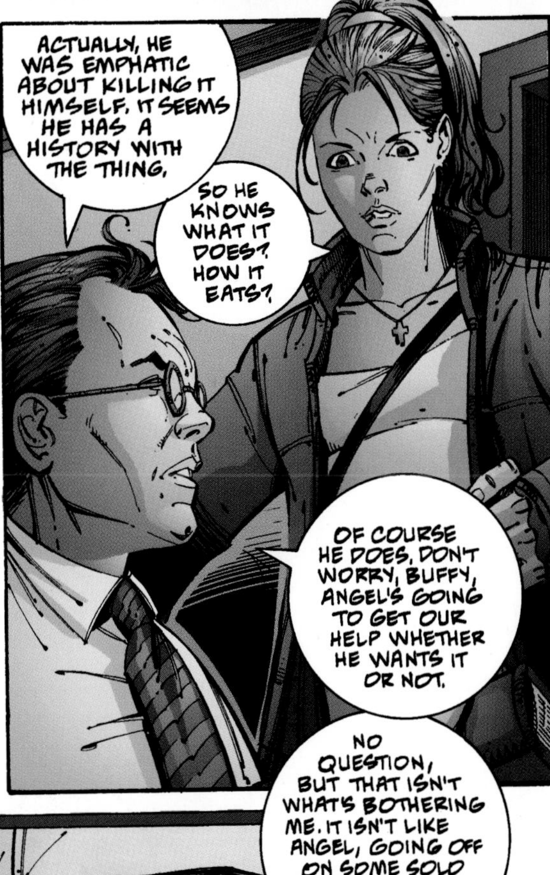

ACTUALLY, HE WAS EMPHATIC ABOUT KILLING IT HIMSELF. IT SEEMS HE HAS A HISTORY WITH THE THING.
SO HE KNOWS WHAT IT DOES? HOW IT EATS?
OF COURSE HE DOES. DON'T WORRY, BUFFY, ANGEL'S GOING TO GET OUR HELP WHETHER HE WANTS IT OR NOT.

NO QUESTION, BUT THAT ISN'T WHAT'S BOTHERING ME. IT ISN'T LIKE ANGEL, GOING OFF ON SOME SOLO MISSION WHEN HE KNOWS WE COULD HELP.
MAKES ME WONDER IF THE REASON HE DOESN'T WANT OUR HELP IS BECAUSE HE HAS NO INTENTION OF KILLING THE HOLLOWER.

"SEE, GILES, THE ONLY THING KEEPING A VAMPIRE WALKING AROUND IS THE DEMON INSIDE IT. WHEN THE HOLLOWER SUCKS THAT OUT, THE VAMPIRE IS DESTROYED.
"BUT ANGEL HAS A HUMAN SOUL IN THERE AS WELL.
"THERE'S NO TELLING WHAT WOULD HAPPEN IF THE HOLLOWER SUCKED THE DEMON OUT OF ANGEL. MAYBE EVEN A MIRACLE. MAYBE ALL THAT'D BE LEFT IS A HUMAN BEING.
"MAYBE ANGEL DOESN'T WANT OUR HELP BECAUSE HE WANTS TO FIND OUT."
ALL RIGHT.
LET'S DO IT RIGHT THIS TIME.

Hunting.
Angel's done this before. He remembers it well. Stalking the Hollower.
Tracking the blood scent the demon leaves in its wake.
Sniff... Sniff...
Last time, more than a century before, they'd hunted in a pack, dogged the creature to its lair under old Vienna. This is different.
It's here, somewhere, in the woods on the outskirts of Sunnydale. But the scent is diffuse. They've spread out, trying to get a fix on it.
It's very close now...
ANNGELLLL!
IT'S KILLED THEM ALL, ANGEL! WE'RE THE LAST! IT JUST CAME UP FROM NOWHERE AND SLAUGHTERED THEM! WHERE WERE YOU, ANGEL?

YOU DID IT AGAIN, YOU CREEP! LEFT ME TO THAT THING, JUST LIKE YOU DID IN VIENNA!
GET OFF ME, CATHERINE.
CATHERINE, STOP IT. COME ON. IF THAT THING'S OUT HERE, WE'VE GOT TO--
I SAID--
OFF!
VIENNA WAS A LONG TIME AGO. I'M NOT THAT CREATURE ANYMORE.
NO? TOO BAD WE CAST NO REFLECTION. YOU COULD USE A MIRROR.
I CAN NEVER ESCAPE WHAT I WAS, WHAT I DID. BUT I KNOW THIS. WHEN I FACED THE HOLLOWER THE FIRST TIME, I HAD ONLY MY OWN INTERESTS IN MIND...
...BUT THIS IS DIFFERENT. WHAT I DO NOW, I DO TO SAVE LIVES, TO PREVENT THIS HORROR FROM SPREADING, AND THIS TIME...

...THE HOLLOWER WILL DIE.

Vienna, 1894.
<GEORG, WHAT ARE THEY? DID YOU SEE THEIR FACES? LIKE DEMONS...>
<HUSH, DARLING. HIDE YOUR FACE AND DO NOT SPEAK OF THEM NOW.>
<LORD, SAVE US FROM THIS HORROR. WE TURN OUR FACES TO THE LIGHT, OUR BACKS TO THE SHADOWS, AND WE PUT OURSELVES IN YOUR HANDS.>
<JUST DON'T LOOK, LITTLE ONE. CLOSE YOUR EYES AND THEY CANNOT HURT YOU. COME THE DAWN, WE WILL LEAVE THIS PLACE.>
<I NEVER WANT TO SEE VIENNA AGAIN.>
<NOW, ME FRIENDS, WE TAKE BACK WHAT IS OURS. TAKE BACK THE NIGHT.>
<DEATH TO THE HOLLOWER!>

NO, DAMN YOUR BLACK HEART, DEMON!
KLINK KLINK KLINK KLINK KLINK
ANGELUS! SPIKE, WE MUST HELP HIM!
AND THAT'S JUST WHAT WE'LL DO, PET...
...FOR ALL THE BLOODY GOOD IT'LL DO.

COME NOW, YOU STICKY DARLING. YOU'RE BEING VERY NAUGHTY.
JUST BURN IT, DRU! BLOODY HELL, IT ISN'T A CAT OR SOMETHING!
IT CERTAINLY ISN'T.
I RATHER LIKE CATS.
AND I DON'T LIKE THIS NASTY BEASTIE AT ALL. NOT THE LEAST.
AYE, THAT'S A GOOD LASS. I WAS A WEE BIT CONCERNED YE'D WANT TO TAKE IT HOME, KEEP IT AS A PET.
I'M COMING, SPIKE, MY LOVE.
RIGHT THEN, IF I'D WAITED FOR YOU TO FINISH SAVING ANGEL AND GET 'ROUND TO ME, I'D BE DUST BY NOW. YE SURELY KNOW HOW TO HURT A MAN, DRUSILLA.
NOW, WHERE'S ME PRETTY BAUBLE?
LOOKING FOR THIS?

YE MAY'VE SAVED US ALL.
BRMBLL
ANGEL! HELP ME!
NO, DAMN YE! IT DINNA BREAK THE FIRST TIME, AND LUCK ONLY GOES SO FAR-- GOT IT!
NOOOOO!
SKREEEEEE
NOW, DEMON, WE FINISH IT!
ANGEL, WAIT! YOU COULD DESTROY CATHERINE.
BETTER HER THAN US.

AAIIEEEE
SSSSSSSSSS
SKREEEEEEE
IT'S NOT DEAD, IS IT?
NO, DEAR WILLIAM, I'M AFRAID IT'S NOT. BUT GONE FOR NOW. THAT'LL HAVE TO BE ENOUGH.
WHAT ARE YOU DOING, ANGELUS? YOU CAN'T LEAVE US ALONE. THE MOON FRIGHTENS ME WHEN YOU'RE NOT THERE. THE BLOOD DOESN'T TASTE RIGHT ANYMORE. OH, PET, WHERE ARE YOU GOING?
EAST.
BUT WHAT ABOUT CATHERINE?
SHE'LL HEAL.

REALLY BUFFY, DO YOU HONESTLY THINK ANGEL WOULD ALLOW THIS HOLLOWER TO LITERALLY SUCK THE DEMON FROM WITHIN HIM...

...JUST ON THE OFF CHANCE THAT HE'LL SURVIVE WITH HIS HUMAN SOUL INTACT?
AH, THAT'S GOT IT.

BUFFY?

YES, WELL, PERHAPS YOU OUGHT TO GO AFTER HIM, THEN. JUST IN CASE, OF COURSE. MEANTIME, I'LL SEE IF I CAN'T TRANSLATE THIS RITUAL, FIGURE OUT HOW TO DESTROY THIS BEAST ONCE AND FOR ALL.

IF YOU CAN FIGURE IT OUT, GREAT...
IF NOT... WE'LL DO THINGS THE MESSY WAY.

THIS WAY... WHEN IT CAME AT US, WE WERE JUST ABOUT...
...HERE.
SUNNYDALE
I'M MISSING SOMETHING. THE ROAD IS ON THE OTHER SIDE OF THAT LOT.
SO, WHY ARE THERE SEWER TUNNELS UP HERE?
UNLESS...
UNLESS WHAT?

UNLESS WHAT, ANGEL?
UNLESS THIS. THE DEMON IS SMART. I THOUGHT THERE MIGHT BE A FARM UP THIS WAY.
BUT THE SMELL CAME FROM HERE. THE HOLLOWER KNEW THE STINK FROM THIS PLACE WOULD HELP TO MASK ITS BLOOD-SCENT, MAKE IT HARD FOR US TO TRACK IT.
IT WORKED FOR A WHILE.
SO YOU THINK THIS WAS WHERE IT WAS HIDING OUT BETWEEN ATTACKS?
NOT WAS, THEO.
IT'S HERE.

"...AND HIS EVIL MAY BE HARNESSED LIKE FIRE FROM HEAVEN."
evil may be harnessed
NOW WHAT ON EARTH DOES THAT MEAN?
EXCELLENT. THAT OUGHT TO DO QUITE NICELY.
Hmm. A BIT CRUDE, BUT IT WILL HAVE TO DO.

ANGEL, I'M... I'M AFRAID. WE HAD SO MANY MORE WITH US LAST TIME, AND WE COULDN'T KILL IT THEN.
THAT'S TRUE. BUT THIS TIME, I CAN'T AFFORD TO LOSE.
KRAKK!
SPLOOSH!
NO, ANGEL... I CAN'T DO THIS! I CAN'T!
YAHHHH!
I BURNED MY FINGERS AND MY EYES DOING THE RITUAL TO MIX THIS HOLY POISON, HOLLOWER.

THAT'S THE LAST TIME YOU'LL KILL.
THEO, NOOO! I WON'T DIE, TOO! I WON'T SPEND FOREVER INSIDE THAT DISGUSTIN BLOATED BEAST!
WHY DO YOU CARE, ANGELUSSS? I'M CURIOUS.
OH, YESSS, I REMEMBER YOU. BUT YOU'RE DIFFERENT NOW, AREN'T YOU? I CAN TASTE IT IN THE AIR. BUT, SSSTILL, WHY DO YOU CARE?
THEY'RE ONLY VAMPIRES. AS EVIL AS I AM.
ANGEL ...I'M... SORRY...
I'M NOT HERE FOR THEM, YOU UGLY FREAK. I'M HERE FOR EVERYONE ELSE. I'M HERE TO STOP YOU NOW, BEFORE YOU SPREAD THE EVIL INSIDE YOU ALL OVER THIS TOWN.

OH, COME NOW, ANGELUS. WITH ALL THE EVIL IN THIS PLACE, SURELY THERE'S ROOM FOR JUST A LITTLE...BIT...
NO, CATHERINE, MOVE IT!
...MORE!
SPLURTCHK!
NO, DAMN YOU! THAT'S ENOUGH!
ENOUGH!
OH, NOT NEARLY ENOUGH, I'M AFRAID. IT WOULD BE ALMOST POETIC, DON'T YOU THINK? IF YOU WERE THE LAST ONE, THE MAGIC NUMBER I NEEDED TO TRIGGER THE EXPULSION OF ALL THE EVIL IN ME?
BUT, SADLY, NO. I'M STILL NOT QUITE FULL.

ON THE OTHER HAND...THIS SHOULD BE INTERESTING.
SSSSSS
NOOOO!
NOOO!
IF I'VE SAID IT ONCE, I'VE SAID IT A THOUSAND TIMES--
--NOBODY MESSES WITH MY BOYFRIEND!

THAT GOES HAND-IN-HAND WITH "BUFFY'S FIRST LAW OF DIPLOMACY"...
BUFFY...?
DON'T TICK ME--
UNGHHH!
NOT QUITE, OLD MAN.

"AND NOT EVER AGAIN, IF WE DON'T HURRY. NOW DO JUST AS I SAY, AND MAYBE WE'LL ALL LIVE TO SEE THE DAWN."
FIGURE OF SPEECH, OF COURSE. NOW THEN, THIS IS A CONTAINMENT CIRCLE. IT SHOULD HOLD THE COLLECTED EVIL OF THE VAMPIRE SOULS WITHIN THE HOLLOWER LONG ENOUGH FOR THEM TO DISSIPATE.
"IN A WAY, THIS SPEAR IS ALMOST LIKE A LIGHTNING ROD, TO GROUND OUT THE CHARGE ONCE THE HOLLOWER RELEASES IT.
"WE SHOULD BE ABLE TO FORCE THAT, BY GROUNDING THE OTHER SPEAR IN THE DEMON ITSELF."
"LET ME GET THIS STRAIGHT. YOU WANT ME TO IMPALE THE HOLLOWER WITH THIS?"
PRECISELY.
HELL, GILES, WHY DIDN'T YOU JUST SAY SO?

HHHAKK! Hunnhh! Hunnh. ANGEL ...WHAT DID YOU JUST DO?
"WHAT DID I DO? I WON. WE WON."

I WAS WORRIED, YOU KNOW. WHEN YOU DIDN'T ASK FOR HELP, I THOUGHT... WELL, I MEAN, I WAS KIND OF AFRAID--
I THINK I CAN GUESS WHAT YOU THOUGHT. BUT THAT WASN'T IT. STUPID AS IT SOUNDS, IT JUST FELT LIKE MY FIGHT. AN OLD FIGHT, UNFINISHED BUSINESS. PLUS, I JUST DIDN'T FEEL RIGHT ASKING YOU TO RISK YOURSELF TO SAVE SOME VAMPIRES.
BUT IF YOU'D OST, ANGEL... I ON'T EVEN WANT THINK ABOUT IT. U SHOULD HAVE AITED. TALKED TO S, INSTEAD OF OING OFF ON OME MACHO AMPIRE TRIP."
"THAT ABOUT SUMS IT UP, YEAH. BELIEVE ME, I KNOW IT WAS DUMB. IF IT HADN'T BEEN FOR YOU, AND..."
GILES?
THANK YOU.
YES, WELL, YOU'RE QUITE WELCOME. BUT THE NEXT TIME THE POPULATION OF SUNNYDALE IS MARKED FOR POSSESSION BY HIDEOUS BLOODTHIRSTY DEMON SPIRITS, DO TRY TO GIVE US A BIT OF WARNING, WON'T YOU?
I'LL SEE WHAT I CAN DO.

SO, I KNOW WE KINDA TOUCHED ON THIS, BUT I'M NOT DONE WITH THE TOUCHING.
YOU REALLY NEVER THOUGHT ABOUT IT? NEVER WONDERED, EVEN FOR A SECOND, WHAT WOULD HAPPEN IF THE HOLLOWER TORE THE DEMON OUT OF YOU? IF YOUR HUMAN SOUL WOULD STAY?
OF COURSE I THOUGHT ABOUT IT, BUFFY. HOW COULD I NOT? I HAVE DREAMS ABOUT BEING HUMAN, WHAT THAT WOULD MEAN FOR ME. FOR US. THEY'RE GOOD DREAMS.
BUT I WASN'T ABOUT TO GIVE IN TO THE HOLLOWER, TAKE THAT RISK, JUST TO SEE WHAT WOULD HAPPEN.
I'VE GOT TOO MUCH TO LOSE.

Christopher Golden is the award-winning, *L.A. Times* bestselling author, of such novels as *Strangewood* and *Of Saints and Shadows*, and a teen-oriented thriller series whose titles include *Body Bags* and *Thief of Hearts*. He has written eight *Buffy the Vampire Slayer* novels (seven with Nancy Holder), including the upcoming *Sins of the Father*. His comic-book work has included *Wolverine/Punisher*, *The Crow*, *Spider-Man Unlimited*, and many *Buffy*-related projects. As a pop-culture journalist, he has co-written such books as *Buffy the Vampire Slayer: The Watcher's Guide* and *The Stephen King Universe* and won the Bram Stoker Award for editing *CUT! Horror Writers on Horror Film*. Please visit him at *www.christophergolden.com*.

Born in Argentina in 1953, graduated architect Hector Gomez moved to Brazil in 1976, where he lives today. He has worked as an advertising illustrator and his painted work has been exhibited in a number of art galleries in both Brazil and Argentina. Hector's work has been published by a slew of Brazilian and American publishers, including *Paranoia* for Malibu, *Battlestar Galactica* for Maximum Press, and *What-If* for Marvel. After a two year absence from comics, when he found work as an art director for web page design company, *Buffy* is Hector's return to the American comic-book scene.

Between his Tibetan yoga and steady diet of ice cream, inking extraordinaire Sandu Florea has made a name for himself working on some of the top books in the industry. Besides current stints on *Blade* and *Conan*, Sandu's talents have graced the pages of *Captain America*, *Thor*, and *The Avengers*. The work on *Buffy the Vampire Slayer* is well suited for Sandu, considering he was born and raised in a small mountain village in Transylvania, a mere ten miles from Dracula's castle.

An interview with
JEFF MATSUDA

by SCOTT ALLIE

I've been working at Dark Horse since 1994, and still don't know how to use the phones. If someone I'm talking to wants to get forwarded to someone else on our same phone system, I tell them to hang up and call that person back. I can handle computers, but these phones are a mess. There's a record option on our phones, and while no one can tell me how it happened, I accidentally recorded the following conversation with Jeff Matsuda, the cover artist on *The Hollower* as well as many of the covers on the current ongoing series, which I thought would make an interesting feature here. For anyone who wanted to know what goes on between the artist and the editor, here you go — with my apologies.

Hey Jeff, it's Scott.

What's up, man?

Did you fix the cover for *Angel* #8 yet?

Actually, no. Jon's sending it to me, I'll be getting it tomorrow night. I'll be doing all the changes.

Okay. Cool.

So you can see it as quick as possible.

Hey, when is the first *Blood of Carthage* cover coming out?

It comes out in May, and Guy hasn't even colored the first cover yet.

He's doing so much work. He's coloring three monthly books for Dark Horse, plus a bunch of covers, plus side projects for Dark Horse, and then stuff for other publishers.

That's a lot of color.

Colorists make more money than anyone else in comics right now. They get like a hundred to a hundred fifty bucks a page.

Which is twice what I make for every cover and every interior page.

Is that right? We'll give you a raise, I promise.

Cool.

[Jeff did the covers for the *Hollower* series, shown on these pages, as well as many of the covers for the current ongoing monthly series.]

[Jeff routinely sends covers to inker Jon Sibal before they're approved, meaning they need to be sent back to him for any changes.]

[*Blood of Carthage* is the story arc running in *Buffy* #21 through #25. Jeff did the covers.]

[Guy Major colored this series, except for the first cover, as well almost every *Buffy* comic Dark Horse has produced.]

[This is something editors tell artists quite often.]

You should go work for Guy. And you know his wife, Chynna, she's doing something in *Blood of Carthage*. We're doing a flashback of Willow, and Chynna's drawing that.

[*CBG*, or *Comics Buyer's Guide*, one of the most popular publications about comics, ran an article about *Buffy* comics in January, 2000, with interviews with Joss and Doug Petrie.]

Have you seen the latest *CBG*?

No.

Joss did an interview. He was talking about how in the comic we don't have the same restraints with the budget as the TV show.

Right.

[Chris Golden is currently writing *Buffy*, and co-writing *Angel* along with Tom Sniegoski.]

I was talking to (Chris) Golden this morning about it. Like in *The Hollower*, Golden wanted to do part of the story in San Francisco, but they wanted to keep it in Sunnydale. We had to keep everything in Sunnydale, because in the show, everything stays in Sunnydale. So in the comic we had to do the same thing, but now Joss is saying no, the comic should have the freedom to go wherever it wants to go. So we should be able to do that.

That is so cool, that Joss is a comics fan.

Yeah. Joss kind of goes off about different comic-book stuff he doesn't talk about in interviews outside of comics. If he starts talking about *Legion of Super-Heroes* and that kind of stuff in *Premiere* or *Entertainment Weekly*, nobody's gonna know what he's talking about. But, in the *CBG*, he knows he can go on and on about that stuff and the readers will get it.

I had a chance to talk to them when I went to the set.

You did?

I did.

You *did*?

I did.

Oh, I didn't think you did.

Yeah, I did.

Did they have that framed artwork hanging up?

[In 1999 we gave Joss the framed cover art to *Angel: The Hollower* #1 as a gift.]

He has the *Angel* cover in his office. Well, I didn't see the office. I saw him outside and we talked a little bit. It was a blast. The sets are incredible.

You know, you still never sent me a picture — one of the pictures that you took from Buffy's bed.

[As soon as the editor receives the picture of Jeff in Buffy's dorm-room bed, it will appear in the *Buffy* letter column.]

Oh, we took a bunch of pictures. You know, in that month, I saw Sarah Michelle Gellar twice.

I know, at the Gene Simmons party, right? When was the other time you saw her?

[Gene Simmons, bass player for KISS, can teach you everything you need to know about rock 'n' roll.]

On the set.

So what's the next batch of craziness?

Golden and I are talking about doing a *Buffy/Angel* crossover. They've done the crossovers on the TV show

but they haven't done, like, a really meaningful one yet. I mean the one where Buffy came to L.A. and —

Buffy came to L.A. and they slept together. That's not meaningful to you?

Well, it was, but they erased it. You know, it was like —

It never happened.

I'd like to see a really big vampire story running through both shows.

Golden wants to do a big vampire gang-war epic.

Like *West Side Story*, but between vampires.

Exactly.

There's some kind of pow wow going on outside my office. It looks like a bunch of scheduling and production people are waiting to kick my ass. But you're gonna get that *Angel* cover back from Jon tomorrow, to fix up a little bit?

Yeah, I'll have it back by tomorrow.

And then fax it to me.

pencils by JEFF MATSUDA, *inks by* DANNY MIKI, *colors by* GUY MAJOR

Why don't I send it to you?

First you gotta pencil it, then Jon has to ink it.

Yeah, right.

Then it goes to a colorist.

Okay.

Well, now that we got that little Comics 101...

It's always hard to remember. A lot of times I send blank pages to inkers.

If you had Kevin Nowlan inking your stuff, you wouldn't have to do any pencils.

No, no, and it'd still look better than even my best drawings, which is the sick part of it. Well, my friend, don't let them hurt you. A lot of it's about looking tough.

Really?

Yeah.

All right. Talk to you later.

Bye.

Bye.

End of recording.

pencils by JEFF MATSUDA, inks by DANNY MIKI, colors by GUY MAJOR

[Kevin is the genius behind Jack B. Quick in Alan Moore's *Tomorrow Stories*.]

Dark Horse Comics: **Mike Richardson** *publisher* • **Neil Hankerson** *executive vice president* • **Andy Karabatsos** *vice president of finance* • **Randy Stradley** *vice president of publishing* • **Chris Warner** *editor in chief* • **Michael Martens** *vice president of marketing* • **Anita Nelson** *vice president of sales & licensing* • **David Scroggy** *vice president of product development* • **Cindy Marks** *director of production & design* • **Mark Cox** *art director* • **Sean Tierney** *computer graphics director* • **Dale LaFountain** *vice president of information technology* • **Kim Haines** *director of human resources* • **Darlene Vogel** *director of purchasing* • **Ken Lizzi** • *general counsel*